QWIK CUTTER

EVAN JACOBS

WH⚡TE L⚡GHTNING BOOKS

BREAK AND ENTER

IGGY

ON THE RUN

QWIK CUTTER

REBEL

SCRATCH AND SNITCH

SADDLEBACK
EDUCATIONAL PUBLISHING
www.sdlback.com

ISBN-13: 978-1-68021-106-1
ISBN-10: 1-68021-106-4
eBook: 978-1-63078-423-2

Printed in Guangzhou, China
NOR/1015/CA21501554

20 19 18 17 16   1 2 3 4 5

STATS OF SHAWN MILLER'S TARDINESS

HOW MANY TIMES SHAWN HAS BEEN LATE TO CLASS THIS WEEK

||||/ ||

HOW MANY TIMES SHAWN HAS BEEN IN TROUBLE FOR BEING LATE → **O**

11:43 PM

TIME SHAWN STARTS HIS HOMEWORK

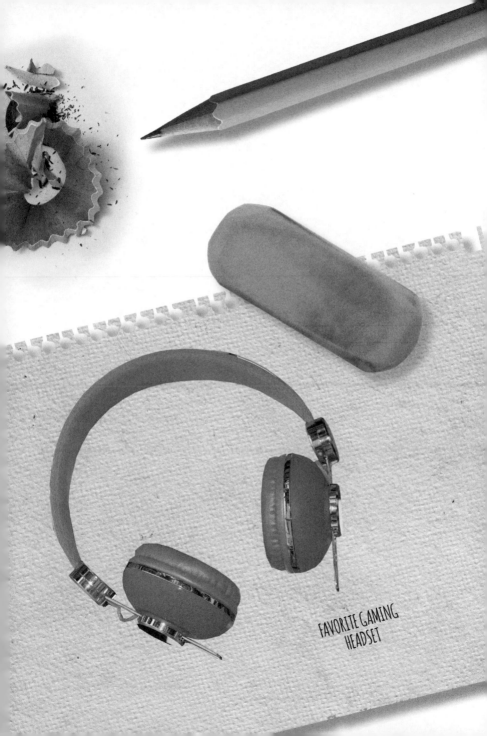

FAVORITE GAMING
HEADSET

CHAPTER 1

FADE-IN

Get to class!" EJ's voice boomed.

EJ was the head security guard at Cube Middle School. He was tall and muscular. He wore workout clothes every day.

Seventh grader Shawn Miller always heard his voice. If you were outside when class started, you always heard it. You could be anywhere on campus. Some students said they could hear it inside the classrooms too.

Shawn was outside when class started. He was always late.

Today he had to stay behind after second period. He needed extra time to do his math test. He was unorganized. And he started the test late. By the time he got going, some kids were done.

Shawn's third-period class was Advanced Video Production.

He loved it. He loved making movies. His favorite ones were horror films. He wanted to be a director someday. But he knew he would have to be more organized to see his dream come true.

Mr. Murphy, the video production teacher, was cool. He directed music videos when he wasn't working at Cube. He also uploaded his videos. The students could watch them on YouTube.

Still, as cool as he was, even Mr. Murphy got tired of Shawn always being late.

Shawn gritted his teeth as he sprinted across campus. He was sweating through his black T-shirt.

He hated that his second- and third-period classes were on opposite ends of the school.

Mr. Murphy won't care about that, he reminded himself.

Somehow he got to video production with five seconds to spare.

He barely heard anything Mr. Murphy said all period. He was working on his science homework. It was due next period. It was assigned three days ago. But that didn't matter. He was always late.

He liked the subject. Wormholes.

He loved anything having to do with time travel. He loved learning about outer space. One day, he hoped to make a movie about it. He even wanted to shoot the movie in space.

Shawn eyed the clock. *Five more minutes,* he told himself.

He just had a few more science questions to complete.

"Don't forget," Mr. Murphy said. "Your summer projects are due tomorrow."

This news normally made students groan. But this wasn't English class. Nobody in Advanced Video Production complained about projects. They all loved being in this class.

"You can either upload them tonight. Or turn them in on a DVD. Or a flash drive. Or an SD card."

"Summer project?" Shawn blurted out.

He was thankful his table partner, John Gomez, was the only one who heard him. John was Shawn's best friend. They had known each other since fourth grade. They both loved technology and making movies. Shawn loved to shoot movies. John loved to edit. They planned to start a production company someday.

"Yeah," Amanda Nguyen said smartly behind her big black glasses. "Mr. Murphy has only been talking about it since forever. Duh!"

Shawn ignored her. She had always hated him. He had called her "four eyes" for all of first grade. But that wasn't the reason why Amanda disliked him. It was because he never got in trouble. For being unorganized. For being late.

Studying late.

Turning in his assignments late.

Sure, he had to stay after class a lot. But his grades never suffered.

Amanda despised this about him. She was super organized. She was on top of things. She was always on time. Always first to raise her hand.

The bell rang. Class was over.

"Have you started editing your project?" Shawn asked John.

"Yeah," John said as he slid his iPad into his backpack. "Haven't you?"

"What do you think?" Amanda snapped before he could answer. "Does Shawn Miller ever do anything on time? Does he ever do anything without having to be reminded to do it a million times?"

Amanda turned and left in a huff.

Shawn was used to her insults. He didn't say

anything back. He didn't have anything to say anyway.

"We shot all that footage over the summer," John said as he headed for the door. "You mean you haven't even started cutting it?"

"It was assigned too early," Shawn said. He walked out of the class with John. "I forgot about it."

"Well, it's due tomorrow. What are you gonna do?"

"I'll get it done." Shawn said confidently. "I always get it done."

LATE BIRD

Shawn was late to fourth period. He didn't plan to be. He never planned to be late. He just was.

He'd been sitting on the bench outside his fourth-period science class.

He didn't have much more homework to finish. Just a few questions left. Still, he couldn't stop thinking about the video production assignment he hadn't started. He had been too deep in thought.

He'd been thinking about wormholes. Then

he thought about how he wanted to edit his video production project. Then he thought about how cool it would be if he could go back in time.

He started imagining himself in the Middle Ages. Next he imagined himself getting one of the first Apple computers. Then ...

"Uh, Shawn." Mrs. Marcel, his science teacher, stuck her head outside the classroom. "If you'd like to join us? Class started twenty minutes ago."

Mrs. Marcel was short. She always wore a pantsuit. She had a stern face, but she was really nice.

Like a lot of the teachers, she seemed to let him slide. She knew when he did his work, he did it well. He got good grades. It just took him a while to get there.

All of the students stared at Shawn as he walked into science class. Many of them smiled and laughed at him.

Shawn just fell further behind from there.

Mrs. Marcel had him stay after class. He had forgotten about the pop quiz. Thankfully, the questions were easy. They were part of the homework assignment he'd just completed.

You still remember this stuff. It's so easy.

This was how things always worked out for him. It was why he never made an effort to get ahead. He never seemed to suffer for being late.

After missing part of lunch, Shawn found John. He was sitting at the lunch tables. He was playing a game of *Clan Castles* on his phone.

"What level are you on?" Shawn asked as he set his lunch tray down.

There were chicken nuggets and french fries on his tray. Shawn's favorite. Too bad he would have to scarf it down. The bell was about to ring.

"Level 35!" John smiled. "Is it true you ditched Mrs. Marcel's class?"

"I didn't ditch." Shawn opened up a packet of ketchup. "I just kinda forgot to go inside the classroom. I was outside doing my homework."

"You're always late," John joked. "Ever since elementary school. Remember how mad Mr. Wager used get at you?"

"Yeah."

Then Shawn remembered something. English. Fifth period. He had an assignment due.

He opened his backpack. He took out his binder. Inside were questions about his reading project, *1984,* by George Orwell.

He hadn't started answering the questions. But he hadn't read the book either. He took out a pencil. He began to answer the questions.

"What are you doing?" John asked. "You never do homework at lunch."

"I forgot I had to do this," Shawn said.

As he was trying to bluff a response to the fourth question, the bell rang. *Man*, he thought. *I have no time today.*

He scooped up his food and his backpack. Then headed to fifth-period English.

Sadly, he only turned in half the assignment.

Mr. Caron wasn't too upset. He didn't yell. Shawn knew he was frustrated by how he shook his head.

Amanda was the worst. The way she smiled smugly at him. The way she seemed to enjoy it when he disappointed people.

Shawn sat in the family room at home. He was playing *Assassin's Creed* on his Xbox. When he played video games, he got into them. Really into them.

His problem wasn't only that he loved video games. His problem was that he loved *all* video games.

He could play *Call of Duty* just as easily as he could play *The Legend of Zelda*. He loved being in other worlds.

He followed all the talk about new virtual reality games. And he was beyond excited.

"When those come out," Shawn would tell his friends. "I'm gonna be gone. I'll have no reason to be here at all."

His eyes were wide as he moved through *Assassin's Creed*. When he was in the zone, he could concentrate. He was the king of video games. None of his friends were better. They liked the games. But Shawn wanted to live them.

"Shawn!" his mom yelled from the kitchen. "Dinner."

He ignored her and continued to play.

Then he remembered it was Tuesday. They always ate early on Tuesdays. His mom went to a school. She was working on her degree. She wanted to be a teacher.

Bor-ring, Shawn thought as he made his way to the dining room.

His parents were already sitting down. The food had already been plated. They were halfway through the meal.

Shawn tried not to look at his parents as he sat down. He didn't want to see their angry faces.

He eyed his full plate. It was pasta with meat

sauce. Not his favorite. He liked hamburgers. But he wasn't going to complain.

"Are you ever on time for anything?" his dad asked.

"Yeah. The movies." Shawn started to eat. He figured his dad wouldn't yell at him if his mouth was full of food.

"The movies," his dad repeated. He was still wearing his suit. He wore one to work every day.

Shawn's mom was casually dressed. She was in school with a lot of younger people. He'd heard her tell her friends that she didn't want to "look like a grandma."

"Have you finished your homework?" his mom asked.

"Yes," Shawn lied.

He had homework in almost every subject. All of it would have to wait. He had to get his video project done.

"You can't be late your whole life," his dad

said. "You continue this way? You're going to get behind. Eventually, you'll be so far behind you'll be forgotten."

"Okay. Um. I'll do better," Shawn said. He took a sip of his juice. *Yeah, right!* he thought. *I'm only thirteen. I still have plenty of time to catch up.*

CHAPTER 3

REALLY BEHIND

I can't believe you're lagging like this." John laughed at Shawn. "Just use iMovie. It will put it together for you."

They were video chatting. Shawn was using his computer. They were searching the Internet for free editing apps. John was on his iPad. Shawn should have been on his iPad too. But he left it at school.

"I know," Shawn said as he searched the net. "I could drop everything into it. We use it in class all the time. But Mr. Murphy will know I did that. I wanna use something else."

"Why are you even in video production?" John asked. "You don't want to make the videos."

"You sound like Amanda. I wanna make them. I just got busy."

"Wait, I found an app. It's called *Qwik Cutter*," John said.

"Link me," said Shawn. He loved tech. He especially loved how editing allowed him to create movies exactly how he wanted.

A link showed up in his messages. He clicked on it.

"Oh, wait. Don't click that link," John said as the page was loading on Shawn's end. "It's a timed program."

"So, I can't keep it?" Shawn eyed the download. All he had to do was click it. Then the program would be his.

"It's only good for twenty-four hours. Unless you buy the full version, all your files will be deleted. Besides, this version looks bad. Hacked. Don't touch it."

Shawn navigated to the *Qwik Cutter* website. He looked at the program specs. *Wow! This app looks awesome.*

It had cool filters. He could add colors he didn't know existed. It allowed users to make crazy transitions. He'd never seen anything like it before.

The best part?

The makers of the app said it was the fastest video editor on the market. Shawn was so behind on his assignment. This would catch him up. He was sure of it. He might even be able to get some of his other homework done too.

"Even if it is timed, it's worth it," he said.

"What if Mr. Murphy doesn't grade it in time?"

"He'll have twenty-four hours. This looks cool. I wanna learn the program. It's not my fault if Mr. Murphy is too late to watch it."

John let out a big laugh. "Says the guy who's always late." John typed a little more on his computer. "Oh, wait. They don't have *Qwik Cutter* for iPad."

"I left mine at school. Remember? Stop being a hater. You're probably jealous 'cause my project is gonna rule. I'm gonna get started."

"Later," John said.

They both hung up.

Shawn was excited. Now Mr. Murphy's assignment didn't seem like work. He was going to get a good grade. Plus he was going to learn a new editing program.

He downloaded *Qwik Cutter*. An icon appeared on his desktop. A filmstrip and a pair of scissors. There was also a skull and crossbones. It was hacked for sure. But he didn't care.

There was also a timer. It read 24 hrs/00 mins. The countdown started.

Shawn looked at the clock. 6:15 p.m. *Well, I better get started.*

CHAPTER 4

FINAL CUT

You have ten more minutes," Shawn's dad said sternly. "And if you're not in bed, you're going to wish you were."

"I'm almost done. Geez!"

Shawn was loading footage into *Qwik Cutter*. It was going well. He only had a few more clips to go. He had named his movie *Shawn's Awesome Class Project.*

"You really need to get a life, Shawn. This

isn't healthy. The computer screen is glued to your face. You need to be outside more."

His dad had said this a million times.

"Dad, you're only saying that because when you were my age, there was nothing to do. Except going outside. It was all you had." Shawn looked up at his dad. "Everybody is on the computer now. I'm not just on it for fun. This is for school. My project is due."

"Well," his dad said. "I think it was better when I was a kid." He turned and walked down the hall.

"Old people always think that," Shawn said under his breath.

He got his last clip in. He looked through all the film clips. There were some of him at Disneyland. The beach. Going to the megaplex to see a movie for the fifth time.

In the last clip, Shawn and John were at the park. Shawn was wearing his Captain America T-shirt.

The clips were lined up. There was a timeline.

A menu came up.

[INDIVIDUAL]

[RANDOM]

He selected RANDOM.

He wished he had more time. The program would now add whatever fades and dissolves it wanted between his clips.

If he had more time, he could pick each one. Individually. He hoped this hacked version wouldn't disappear. He wanted to use it on one of his own projects.

Another menu appeared.

[EDIT]

[QWIK CUT]

He selected QWIK CUT.

A time bar popped up. It said it would take forty minutes to export.

Plenty of time, he thought. He yawned, realizing how tired he was. *I'll upload it tomorrow.*

Shawn eyed the clock. It was a little after ten.

He looked at how much time the program would keep working. How long would it be before it disappeared from his computer. It read 20 hrs/15 mins.

No worries. This is awesome. Shawn grinned. Then he went to bed. For some reason his pillow never felt so good. His bed never felt so soft. Shawn fell asleep before he could have another thought.

🕛

That night he had a dream. It wasn't a normal dream. It was nothing like any he'd ever had.

This was like he was the star of a movie. One of his movies. It looked like it was shot on video. There were fades. Ripple effects. And filters on the footage.

Shawn was moving through it.

It opened with the first piece of footage he had put into *Qwik Cutter*.

Shawn and John at Disneyland. This had been the first day of summer vacation. They were walking through the park. It looked awesome. Shawn loved being lost in his footage.

But something weird happened. Every time he moved past anything, it vanished. Then all he could see were 0s and 1s. This was the binary code for digital information.

By the time his clip was done, everything in the Magic Kingdom was gone.

The next clip was shot at the beach. As he moved through the scene, the beach began to disappear! All the sand. All the water. All the people. Gone.

This kept happening in all the clips.

Shawn moved through the last clip. It was from the park near his house. John turned into code!

"John!" Shawn called.

It was too late.

His best friend was gone.

Shawn looked around.

The park had disappeared. The grassy hills. The basketball courts. The playgrounds. The 0s and 1s would soon engulf him.

Wake up! he told himself.

He looked at the ground. He saw his reflection in a puddle. As the puddle disappeared, he realized he was disappearing too. Turning into 0s and 1s.

And then everything went black.

He didn't wake up. He was still dreaming.

"Hello?" he said out loud. But nobody answered.

CHAPTER 5

PARK?

Shawn felt wet. Like he had water all over him.

Sometimes he drooled when he slept. It didn't feel like that today. It felt like he was sleeping in a puddle.

"What the?" he said as he opened his eyes.

What was happening? He was at the park!

"How did I get here?!" he screamed. He sat up quickly.

The early morning sun slowly warmed the

air. It looked exactly as it did in his dream. But it wasn't turning into 0s and 1s.

He wore the same clothes he had worn in his film. He was in his Captain America T-shirt and jeans.

It's like I'm back in the clip I loaded into the program last night, he thought. *But how did I get here? I wasn't wearing these clothes yesterday.*

He pinched himself. He heard if you were dreaming and did that, you'd wake up. He didn't go anywhere. Nothing changed.

Shawn looked around the park. He had a lot of questions. None of this made sense.

So he decided to go home.

CHAPTER 6

HOME UNKNOWN

Shawn smiled as he walked up to his house. Going home was normally no big deal.

That wasn't the case this morning.

How did I get from my bedroom to the park? he asked himself. *Is there something wrong with me? Maybe I'm sick. Maybe I was sleepwalking.*

His parents always yelled at him for sitting too close to the TV. For being too close to the computer. For spending too much time in front of screens.

What if I get in trouble? Wait! I didn't go to the park. Not willingly anyway.

This was too weird.

He walked up to the front door. He took out his key. And put it in the lock. He turned the key. The lock didn't budge.

"What? Hey!" he said out loud.

Then he realized his key not working was maybe a good thing.

"I was outside when I wasn't supposed to be," he said.

He decided to go around back. His parents had a two-story house. They always left the sliding glass door unlocked. He planned to sneak in that way. Maybe they wouldn't even notice he had been gone.

Shawn rounded the corner of the house.

That's when he almost had a heart attack.

Through the sliding glass door, he saw something he didn't understand. His parents were downstairs. They were eating breakfast like usual. Sitting across from them appeared to be a thirteen-year-old girl.

A girl? What?

"Okay!" a frustrated Shawn screamed. "What's going on here?"

He thought it must be a joke. Maybe his parents were trying to teach him a lesson. Or something. They were tired of how much he played video games. Of how he was always on the computer. Of how he was always late.

Everybody inside the house looked at him.

His heart sank.

They didn't know him. He could tell. Their faces were blank.

"What are you doing in our backyard?" his dad screamed. He ran toward the glass door.

The thirteen-year old girl screamed.

Shawn's mother looked too surprised to move. "Call the police!" she said.

"The police? Wait! I live here," Shawn yelled.

Realizing it didn't matter, he ran. He didn't slow down until he was blocks away.

CHAPTER 7

SCHOOL SWEET SCHOOL

It wasn't until Shawn was calm again that he saw something.

Students. Walking to school.

I never thought I'd think this. But I should go to school.

He watched people he knew. They just walked past him.

Huh. They never see me this early, he thought. *Maybe that's why nobody's saying anything.*

As he watched them go by, he saw their backpacks.

All my stuff's at home. He didn't want to go to school without anything. *I can't go back there. Not right now anyway.*

He thought about his options. He could do nothing all day. Just walk around town. Snooze!

His mind started working overtime. He imagined himself being one hundred years old. He still couldn't go home. He was still walking around town. A total stranger.

I'm going to school.

He started walking behind the other kids.

"Excuse me, young man," EJ said in his loud voice.

Shawn looked at him.

The security guard wasn't smiling. Usually when EJ talked to Shawn, he smiled. It was his way of getting kids to stay in line. They also knew he was serious at the same time.

"Where are you going?"

Shawn continued to stare at the guard. Then he realized EJ didn't know who he was.

"EJ … um … sir," he said. "It's me. Shawn Miller. I'm the kid who's always late."

But he wasn't late today. He was on time.

EJ didn't recognize him at all.

"New students go to the office." EJ pointed. "Did your parents drop you off?"

"You *really* don't know me?" Shawn tried to smile. "I'm the kid who is never on time. You're always telling me to hurry up. I know this school like the back of my hand. I've been here since last year. When I started middle—"

"Look," EJ said. His tone was firm. The last thing Shawn needed was to get in trouble. "I know this school like the back of my hand too. Even more, I know all the students. And I don't know you, Mr. …?"

"Miller."

"Well, Mr. Miller," EJ said, placing his hand on Shawn's shoulder. "Let's go. We'll get to know the front office."

Shawn didn't have to do that. He knew everybody there. He'd gotten more tardy notes than he could count. Though he'd never gotten in big trouble.

Today? Shawn had a feeling his luck had run out.

⚡

"Listen," Shawn said as he sat across from Principal Bennett. "My name is Shawn Miller. Nobody seems to recognize me today. Not you. Not EJ. Not even my own parents."

Principal Bennett was tall. He had a thick head of blond hair. Some days he wore neckties. Other days he wore Hawaiian shirts.

Shawn had never had a problem with him.

Until today.

Shawn had never actually had any problems till today.

"So?" Principal Bennett looked at him. "You went to bed. Then woke up in the park?"

"Yeah, basically. That's right."

Principal Bennett stared at him. Like EJ, Shawn could tell he didn't believe a word.

He was getting tired of this. He was getting tired of the weird looks. He just wanted to go to class. Then he wanted to go home. Like a normal kid.

He'd always been behind. Late. Slow. But today?

He was *really* behind. He didn't shower that morning. Or eat breakfast. He hadn't been able to go to class.

"Okay." He knew he needed to tell the whole truth. "I downloaded this program called *Qwik Cutter*. I was behind in my Advanced Video Production class. A project is due. The program was hacked," he said. "I wasn't cheating or anything. I just wanted to use a program Mr. Murphy wouldn't know. It did all the work for me. I loaded my video footage into it. The program was really cool. When I went to bed, it was finishing up. When I woke up, it was like I wasn't in my life anymore. "

Then Shawn put it together.

Principal Bennett continued to stare at him. He looked confused.

"Sir, don't you see what's happened?"

"No, young man. I don't," the principal replied.

"It's that program. *Qwik Cutter*. Somehow it has edited me out of my own life!"

CHAPTER 8

INVISIBLE MAN

They think I'm crazy, Shawn told himself.

After talking with Principal Bennett, he was sent to the school nurse.

She examined him. "You don't have a fever," she said.

I know that, he wanted to scream. He didn't. He had a feeling his weird morning would morph into an even weirder day.

After the nurse, he spoke to the school psychologist. Her name was Ms. Kennedy.

All she did was ask him a lot of questions.

What did he do after school?

What were his interests?

Was he happy?

Did he have a lot of friends?

It wasn't until almost eleven o'clock that he went to his first class.

Fourth-period! Shawn couldn't believe it. *I'll never catch up today.*

As he sat around kids he had known since kindergarten, he was sad. None of them knew him.

He hadn't seen John yet. But he figured John wouldn't know him either.

Making it even worse, he didn't have his old schedule. The office wouldn't give it to him. Not even when he told them his routine.

There was a bright side. Mrs. Erickson, his new fourth-period English teacher, was really nice. She didn't know anything about him. She didn't know he was always late. That his assignments were always turned in after the due date.

Maybe I can start over, he thought. *Wait! What are you thinking? You've lost your life. You have to get it back.*

He tried to focus on English. It was no use. He had a different teacher. His class had already read *The Outsiders*.

I don't even have video production. He wanted to cry. But he didn't. He knew it wouldn't help.

❦

Shawn walked by John Gomez and Mateo Bass at lunch. They both carried their lunches. He waved. Then he remembered. They wouldn't know him.

John made eye contact with Shawn.

"Hey," Shawn said.

"Hey," John replied.

John and Mateo walked past him.

"You know that guy?" Mateo asked.

"No," John said.

"Seemed like he knew you."

They both walked to a table and sat down.

Shawn went and got his lunch. It was free today. The principal had arranged it. But despite not eating breakfast, he wasn't hungry. He was too worried.

What if this is my life? he thought. *What if it never goes back to normal?*

Shawn got a chicken sandwich. Then he took some potatoes and carrots. He thought about sitting with John and Mateo. Then he decided not to.

They don't know me. It'll be too weird.

So he sat alone instead. He managed to eat the potatoes. He even ate some of the carrots. But he didn't feel like eating the sandwich. He wasn't hungry enough. The old Shawn was always starving by lunch. Not today. Not the new Shawn.

He decided to put the sandwich in his pocket. *I'll probably need this later.* He realized it might be all he'd have to eat for dinner.

He sat and stared at the other students. They were having fun. They loved being at Cube

Middle School. He used to feel the same way. Not anymore.

Then he had an idea. *My iPad! I left it in the video production classroom.*

Shawn and John had been working on a project together. It was on his iPad.

Maybe I can find some old footage on it, he thought. *I'll show it to Principal Bennett. I'll show it to John. That'll make them remember me. Shawn Miller, the kid who's always late.*

He stood up and quickly moved across campus. He was determined to get his life back.

CHAPTER 9

DISSED ... SORT OF

The video production classroom was locked.

Shawn remembered Mr. Murphy always locked it between classes.

"There's expensive equipment in here," he'd say. "We're all responsible for it."

Shawn came back after school. He saw Jeff, the janitor, walking out of the classroom with a bucket and mop.

Please don't shut the door, Shawn thought.

Jeff shut the door.

No! Darn!

But he didn't lock it.

Yahoo! A lucky break. Yes! Shawn smiled.

The janitor put the bucket and mop down. He walked over to the restrooms.

Shawn ran into the classroom. He made his way over to his seat. He was filled with excitement.

If my iPad is still here, I can prove I'm Shawn Miller. Everything will go back to normal. I'll never use that app again. Ever!

Shawn found his desk. All the desks had a tote tray. That's where he'd left his iPad.

Here goes nothing, he thought. He took a deep breath. He opened his tote tray.

An iPad was in there!

He pulled it out. There was a sticker on it. It said *AN*.

"*A-N?*" Shawn said out loud.

"Hey," a voice called from the door. "Put my iPad down!"

Shawn looked over. There was Amanda. She was standing in the hallway. He saw her eyes burning with anger. Even with those black glasses on.

He didn't know what to do. He would have been sad if he wasn't so confused about everything.

"Shawn Miller!" she said. "I told you to put my iPad down. I'm gonna tell the principal."

She knew him? "Okay." Shawn opened up the tote tray. He gently slid it inside. "Here it is. I'm sorry. I thought it was mine."

"Why would you think it was yours? Because you only think about yourself? Because you're always late? Because you think you can do whatever you want? Because you get away with everything?"

Amanda moved the big glasses. She seemed like she wanted to get a better look at this person she disliked.

Normally, Shawn would have been mad. But not today. "You know me. I can't believe it. You know me!" He smiled. Then laughed.

"Of course I know you," Amanda shot back. "You're Shawn Miller. You've been late since you were born."

"Well," he said. "You're gonna think this is totally crazy. But …"

He proceeded to tell her his story. He knew he didn't have a lot of time. He knew she was going to think he was crazy.

Still, Amanda was his only hope to get his life back.

When he was done, Amanda stared at him. "Do you think I'm stupid?" she finally asked.

"No, I just—"

"Look, Shawn." Amanda put her hands on her hips. "I'm not gonna play these childish games. You've been acting weird all day. You didn't show up to class."

"They wouldn't let me," he protested.

"And now you're in here trying to steal my iPad."

"I wasn't trying to steal it." He was trying to keep his cool. It wasn't easy.

"You're acting all surprised that I know you. Look. Stop. Just stop. Your games may work with everyone else. But they don't work with me."

"Amanda?" Shawn felt like he might start crying. That would be the worst. He didn't want to cry in front of someone who didn't like him.

"I don't have time to listen anymore. You've wasted enough of my time. My mom is picking me up."

With that, she took her iPad and walked out of the classroom.

Shawn started to follow her.

As he did, the janitor walked into the classroom. "You're not supposed to be here," he said. "School's over for the day."

"I know," Shawn said. "I get it. I'm not supposed to be anywhere today."

He walked out of the room. He saw Amanda

walking toward the front of the school. Her mom was waiting for her in her white minivan.

He moved fast. Faster than he thought he could ever move. *Maybe if I appeal to her mom ... She might force Amanda to help me.*

He knew it was a long shot. But he went after her.

As usual, he was too late. By the time he got to the front of the school, the minivan was gone.

"Great," he said. He felt like crying. *Where am I gonna go? What am I gonna do till school starts tomorrow?*

He looked around.

That was when he saw Principal Bennett walking toward him.

He may have had nowhere to go, but that was better than what Principal Bennett probably had in mind.

Before the principal could get any closer, Shawn took off.

CHAPTER 10

PROOF

Shawn knew Amanda was the only person who could help him.

I can't give up on her. He felt weird thinking that.

Yesterday? She had been his number one enemy. Today? She might be the only person who could help him get his old life back.

So he went to her house. He didn't knock on the door. He knew if he did, her mom would ask a lot of questions. Or even worse, Amanda would answer the door. Then she'd slam it in his face. Or she might refuse to speak with him at all.

He decided to wait outside. There was a large tree across from her house. Despite being totally depressed, he felt good in the shade.

As he stared at Amanda's house, he remembered the last time he was there. It was fifth grade. Amanda's tenth birthday. He showed up two hours late. He hadn't even brought a gift.

Amanda never invited him to another party.

Shawn had also teased her when they were younger.

I shouldn't have done any of that, he thought. *Man, if I can get back to my old life? I promise I won't be late anymore. And I'll be nicer to people. I will. Especially to Amanda.*

Then he heard a click. The door to Amanda's house opened.

She came outside. She went to the mailbox. She started taking out the mail.

Shawn walked over to her. He realized he must've looked crazy. But he didn't care.

"Amanda," he called.

She looked at him. In an instant her expression turned to disgust.

"Look, Shawn, I'm tired of this joke you're playing on me."

"It's no joke. I promise you, Amanda. It's a matter of life and death."

"Yeah, right." She crossed her arms.

At that moment John rode by on his bicycle.

"Watch this," Shawn said. He turned to his best friend. "John!"

John stopped riding his bike. But he didn't come over to them.

"Yeah?"

"What's my name?" Shawn asked.

"I don't know, dude." John smiled a little. Then he rode off.

"Very funny. You guys probably set that up. Having him ride by at exactly the right time."

"We didn't," Shawn said. "I swear. He's not coming back." He stared at John's back.

Amanda watched Shawn.

John kept riding. Eventually, he was gone.

"He's not coming back," Amanda said, confused.

"Do you believe me now?"

"No." But she didn't sound too sure.

"I have an idea," he said.

"What?"

"You're not in any of these," Amanda said as they flipped through some old yearbooks. They looked at one from Cube Middle School. Then they looked at all the ones from their elementary school.

They were sitting in her bedroom. It was very neat and organized. The total opposite of Shawn's. Her shoes were sitting by the bed. Amanda's backpack was hanging off a chair. She had a bookshelf full of nonfiction books. On her desk was a picture of her and her parents.

"I told you. Now do you believe me?"

Amanda eyed the yearbooks. She shook her head. "Yeah. I guess." She shut a yearbook. "So, wait. You're so bad you're not just late anymore. The universe got its revenge. You're not even here."

"I know. It's awful. I told you this is the worst day of my life," he said sadly. He was relieved she believed him.

"How are we going to get you back? That footage you had of your summer doesn't even exist anymore." Amanda started to collect her yearbooks.

"We might be able to. Do you have any money in your iTunes account?" He had an idea. A new way to get back his life back.

⚡

"Well," Amanda said a while later. She was sitting in front of her computer. "I bought the full *Qwik Cutter* program. You owe me thirty dollars."

"That's fine. I'll pay you back. If this works," Shawn said.

"But I still don't understand how it helps. We don't have any of your old footage."

"Maybe we do"

"How?"

"Well, when I went to bed, the file was exporting. I had planned to upload it the next day. Today. Then I had a dream about the footage. The images were disappearing into zeros and ones."

"The binary code for everything digital," Amanda said. "Ah."

"Exactly. Hey, maybe there's some footage still on my computer." He started to think he might really have a chance. A chance to resume his old life.

"Why would there still be footage on that computer? You have a new life now, remember?" Amanda adjusted her glasses.

"I don't know. Maybe it's there. Maybe this is my punishment for using the hacked version of *Qwik Cutter*. Maybe this is the universe's way of telling me to do things the right way for once. And not always last minute."

Amanda stared at him.

Despite her disgust for his behavior, he felt she really wanted to help. She couldn't help being critical. Not after all he'd done.

"So, how do we get the footage?" she finally asked. "If it's there. And that is a big if. It's in a house you no longer live in."

Shawn realized Amanda was in. They would solve this together. They were a team. He'd never in a million years thought his life would depend on her. He felt like a jerk.

"Don't worry about it being there or not," he said. "What's the largest flash drive you have?"

CHAPTER 11

MISSION IMPOSSIBLE

Shawn and Amanda walked down the street. They were headed to his house. They reviewed his plan.

"So, you'll knock on the door …" he said.

"And I'll say I live on the street behind them," Amanda finished his words. "I'll say I was playing with a ball in my backyard. And it accidentally went into their yard."

"Exactly. This way you can just leave when they don't find the ball. You say you'll check your yard again. While you're talking to them, I'm gonna get inside through the doggy door."

There was a doggy door in the side yard. It would let him into the garage. His family didn't have a dog. But the previous owners must have.

He could fit through the small door. It drove his parents crazy.

"You're going to get stuck in there one day," his mom would say.

"We're not going to help you when you do," his dad would say.

Shawn had always shrugged it off. Nothing bad ever seemed to happen to him. Not until today.

"What if the doggy door isn't there?" Amanda asked.

"It should be." But he wasn't sure.

"What if it isn't, genius? Then what?"

Shawn knew she didn't like his plan.

"Once I'm inside the house, I'm gonna fly upstairs," he explained.

"Do you remember the layout? What if it's different?" she asked.

"Amanda! Focus! I need you to think positive right now. Please."

Amanda stared at him. She adjusted her glasses.

"Maybe this is why we've always fought. I'm positive. You're negative. Well, not negative. Your glass is half empty. Mine is half full. We just don't mesh."

"Maybe," Amanda sighed.

Suddenly, Shawn felt bad. He didn't mean to hurt her feelings.

"But things are different now. We're working together. We're friends!" He tried to smile. He knew he had to keep being positive.

Amanda smiled uneasily.

"Anyway, I'm gonna run upstairs. I'll go to my room. Fire up my computer. And put the footage on your flash drive. Then we'll take it to your house. We'll edit it so I can get back to my old life."

"If they call the police, I'm blaming you for everything," Amanda said.

"It's gonna work. Remember? Believe and you can achieve." Shawn pumped his fist.

"Just out of curiosity, what time did you start using *Qwik Cutter* last night?" Amanda asked.

"Six fifteen. I remember because the app had a clock on it. Since it was hacked, it also had a skull and crossbones."

"What happens if you don't finish your project by the time the clock runs out?"

Shawn hadn't thought about it. He didn't want to go there. "I don't know. Maybe I will disappear." A chill ran down his spine.

Amanda took out her phone. "Shawn? It's almost five. We've only got a little over an hour."

They turned the corner. Shawn saw his house.

His mom's car was in the driveway. He wondered briefly why she hadn't parked in the garage. His dad would be coming home from work soon.

"Let's do this," he said.

He hid behind a bush as he watched Amanda in action.

She walked up to the front door. Then she knocked on it.

He couldn't hear the conversation. He hoped Amanda was convincing enough. He wanted everyone to go in the backyard. Then he could sneak inside.

After a few moments Amanda walked into the house. The door closed behind her.

Go! Shawn told himself.

He headed over to the side gate. He reached over. Then pulled the latch.

What if they have a lock or something? he thought.

Then he heard a click. The gate opened.

So far so good.

He moved along the wall. He came up to the

side door. He slowly looked down. The doggy door was still there!

Yes! Shawn couldn't help pumping his fist.

If things continued to go his way, he would get his old life back.

He got down on his knees. Then he started crawling through the doggy door. It was tighter than he remembered.

"Ah. Ugh." He tried to be as quiet as possible. It wasn't easy. *I wonder if this is the same doggy door.*

Inside the garage it was dark. His father would be home any minute. He needed to move fast. Before the garage door opened. He kept wiggling his body through the small door.

Then he heard something.

It wasn't his father.

It was low to the ground. Heavy.

He heard sounds on the garage floor.

Click. Click. Click.

It was slow. Then fast. Then super fast.

Not a dog! Shawn thought.

The dog growled as it came closer.

Shawn pushed himself through the doggy door. He scrambled to his feet.

He couldn't really see the dog. He knew it was coming toward him.

Shawn started to run toward the door leading into the house. *I have to get out of this garage*, he thought urgently.

Then he stepped on something. And fell to the floor. He didn't know what had tripped him up. But he didn't have time to think about it.

The dog was barking. Shawn's eyes adjusted to the dim light. The dog was a black Labrador retriever.

"Shhh! Good doggy." Shawn knew the dog wouldn't listen.

It moved toward him. It barked again.

Shawn knew he only had so much time. Eventually, someone would come to check it out.

Getting busted by a sister I don't even have? No way, he thought.

Then he remembered something. The chicken sandwich from lunch. The one he didn't eat. The one in his pocket!

"Want some food? Good dog," Shawn whispered. He tried to be as calm as possible.

He took out the sandwich. Unwrapped it. And threw it near the dog.

It licked its lips. Then it moved over to the food. And started to eat.

Shawn slowly got to his feet. He backed up toward the door to the house.

When the time was right, he quickly opened it and went inside. He moved past the living room. Then he turned and saw the stairs.

The layout of the house was still the same.

As he went upstairs, he saw Amanda. She was in the backyard. His mom and his fake sister were there. They were talking. He couldn't hear the conversation.

He ran up to the second floor. He turned a corner and went into his bedroom.

Shawn took a deep breath. He was shocked. He tried not to faint.

His bedroom was now a girl's bedroom!

The walls were pink. The ceiling was pink. There was princess stuff everywhere.

There were dolls from *Frozen*. American Girl dolls. Who was this girl? She even had a big Olaf plush on her bed.

On his walls—his!—were pictures of his fake sister and her friends.

As if this wasn't horrible enough? There were One Direction posters everywhere. She was a huge fan. It was too much for Shawn. He was overwhelmed.

Block it out! he told himself. *I have to find the computer. Focus on that. Come on!*

He looked for his desk. It wasn't there.

He rushed over to the closet. It was filled with more girlie stuff. Clothes, shoes, hats, purses … no computer.

"No! No! No!" Shawn said out loud.

He didn't care if anybody heard him at that moment. Without his computer there was no footage. Without the footage there was nothing to edit. Without anything to edit he might disappear forever!

He looked at the clock. It was shaped like a heart. He wanted to barf.

5:14 p.m.

Then he remembered something.

His mom and dad had been complaining about all kinds of media. They didn't like how he was always playing video games. They didn't like how he was always on his phone. Or his iPad. He wasn't going outside. He wasn't getting fresh air. Or exercise.

"You kids these days. You're all going to become computer zombies," his mom would say.

Shawn would ignore her. *She always threatened to put my computer in the spare bedroom*, he thought. *I wonder if she ...*

Before he finished his thought, he ran from

his bedroom. He moved down the hall. Toward the guest bedroom.

He took a deep breath and walked in. His fingers were crossed.

It looked normal. Just like it had looked yesterday. But there was a desk. With Shawn's computer on it!

He sighed. Then he gasped. He heard the sliding glass door. The one that led to the backyard.

Yikes! He could hear voices downstairs. Everyone was now inside.

He was running out of time!

CHAPTER 12

DOWN*LONG*

Shawn turned on the computer. It took forever to boot. But the home screen finally came up.

He scanned the hard drive.

The *Qwik Cutter* program was there! There was the skull and crossbones. The timer was still counting down. It read 53 mins/41 secs.

Shawn clicked the app. An editing window opened up. Was his project there? Yes! It looked like it was.

Another window appeared.

FILE NOT FOUND

"What?" he gasped.

He checked the trash. In it was a folder.

SHAWN'S AWESOME CLASS PROJECT

He pulled it out of the trash. He couldn't believe it. His plan might work after all. All he had to do was edit the clips. Use the editing program. The *real* program. The one Amanda purchased. Not the hacked version.

He heard voices coming from downstairs.

He took out Amanda's flash drive. He stuck it into the computer. He grabbed his folder. Dropped it into the drive.

A new window came up.

COPYING TIME 10 MINUTES

Then he heard the front door close. He figured Amanda had left.

He heard footsteps coming up the stairs. They were fast. Too fast!

Too fast for my mom, he thought.

He eyed the computer.

COPYING TIME 6 MINUTES

"Mom," the girl yelled.

Shawn thought she might be upstairs now.

"Where's my copy of *The Outsiders*? I need it for school."

"I think I put it in the spare room."

"Why would you do that?" the girl whined.

Man, Shawn thought. *My parents have a really bratty girl.*

He figured she was spoiled. Maybe always complaining. Always crying about this or that. That s was always—

Then he remembered something.

Whoa! Crap. I'm in the spare room.

He checked the computer.

COPYING TIME 2 MINUTES

He watched in horror as the doorknob turned.

Shawn looked around. The room was small. Too small. There was a tiny space behind the bed.

The door started to open.

He looked at the computer again.

COPYING TIME 1 MINUTE

"Come on," he whispered.

He dove behind the bed. But he was too big. Little Miss Brat would see him for sure. The door was completely open. The girl walked in. She looked right at him.

CHAPTER 13

BINARY DISSOLUTION

Mom? Why is … " the brat started to say.

But then she dissolved into a billion 0s and 1s.

Just like my dream! Shawn thought. He couldn't believe what he was seeing. He knew he wasn't dreaming. He pinched himself. Just to make sure.

Eventually the code disappeared in a puff of smoke.

He didn't know what to do. He just stared at the puff as it disappeared.

No time for this! Get the flash drive, he told himself.

He sprang into action. He moved to the computer.

The copying countdown window was gone. Shawn clicked on the flash drive icon. His folder was there.

He ejected the flash drive. He walked toward the door. He looked around. There was nobody in the hallway.

Shawn started to move. He got to the stairs. He took them one by one. Then he heard something. His mother. She was still in the kitchen. The kitchen was near the front door. There was no way he could get out of the house. His mom would see him.

Why hasn't she turned into code?

He stopped on the last step. Took a deep breath. Then he crept toward the kitchen.

His mom was washing dishes. She turned the water off. Wiped her hands. Then walked toward the dining room.

Shawn knew she wouldn't be able to see him from there. He made a break for the door. He ran as fast as he could.

"*Woof! Woof!*" The dog was inside the house.

Run! Shawn didn't know how close the dog was. But it was too close for comfort. He ran faster.

"Bandit! Bandit," his mom called. "Quiet down!"

Shawn reached the front door. He had to get out of the house. If he didn't, Bandit was going to tear him apart.

The front door began to open before Shawn could turn the lock.

"What is happening?" he asked out loud.

Before he knew it, his dad was standing there.

"Hey, kid!" his dad yelled. "You're the sneak from this morning!"

Shawn slid to his knees. He dove through his father's legs. He was out! He had done it. He jumped to his feet and ran. He was stressed out. His feet picked up speed. He was struggling to breathe.

"*Woof! Woof! Woof!*" The dog was chasing him. It was too fast. It was getting closer. Shawn felt Bandit's breath on his legs.

He closed his eyes. His legs hurt. His lungs hurt. His whole body ached. He forced himself to keep moving.

He felt something hot on his leg. Then something sharp. The dog was biting him!

"Ahhh!" he screamed.

Suddenly, the dog didn't sound close. Shawn couldn't feel its hot, slobbery breath on his legs. He didn't feel the sharp teeth.

I can't look back. I don't have time. I need every second, he said to himself. But he couldn't help it.

The dog had changed into code. All 0s and 1s.

Shawn slowed down. Then he walked. Tried to catch his breath.

"Hey!" a voice called. It was Amanda. She adjusted her glasses. Holding them as she ran over. "We need to get that footage into my computer," she said. "It's past five thirty. We have less than forty-five minutes. We have to get to my house."

She took his hand. And took off. Dragging him behind.

They headed back to her house. As they ran, cars, houses, trees, and even people turned into code. Everything was exploding into the two numbers.

"What's going on?" Amanda couldn't believe what she was seeing. "Everything's disappearing," she yelled.

"It's the program," Shawn said as he gasped for air. "It's just like the dream I told you about. Our time's almost up."

He looked up into the sky. Flying birds dissolved into 0s and 1s.

"We're gonna go too," Shawn said. "It's like we're in an alternate universe. Some binary movie."

He loved tech. Loved making movies. Loved editing. How could something he loved end his life? It wasn't fair.

"You see?" Amanda gripped his hand tighter. She continued to run. "This is why you're always late. You let your mind get sidetracked. We need to get your stupid video project finished. Once and for all!"

DIGITAL DOMAIN

They got to Amanda's house. It was slowly disappearing.

Shawn slowed his paced.

"What are you doing?" Amanda yelled. "Keep going!"

"But—"

"But nothing! Move. Move. Move," she ordered.

They hurried inside. Raced upstairs. Shawn tried not to look behind them. But he couldn't help it.

Actually, he couldn't believe it. The stairs were disappearing as they went up. Turning into 0s and 1s.

"Come on," Amanda screamed. She practically dragged Shawn with her.

They got to the top of the stairs. The house was going before their eyes. Each room started to break into code.

"Shawn!" Amanda waved her hands in front of his face. "You can't always be late. I'm freaking out! We've gotta get to my room."

"What if it's not there anymore?" he asked.

"It has to be there! We have to believe."

They ran into Amanda's bedroom. She tapped her computer keyboard.

The room's walls were almost gone. Sunlight was streaming in.

Shawn inserted the flash drive. He sat down in front of the computer. He clicked on the legal *Qwik Cutter* app.

But the desk started to disappear. It would be gone soon.

Then he noticed the floor was turning into code too.

"Hurry," Amanda screamed. "Come on, Shawn. Please!"

"I am," he said. "I'm not used to moving this fast."

He put the folder from the flash drive onto the desktop.

A window came up.

COPYING TIME 10 MINUTES

"Oh no!" Shawn screamed.

Then the time changed.

COPYING TIME 5 MINUTES

"Come on," Amanda said. She crossed her fingers.

Everything was disappearing. The wall. The floor. The desk. Code was everywhere.

Shawn didn't want to see the numbers. So he

looked at Amanda. She seemed just as nervous as he was. He did the one thing he knew he needed to do.

"Thank you, Amanda," he said.

She looked at him. It was like she couldn't believe what he'd said.

"Thank you for everything. I know you haven't always liked me. I'm sorry about your birthday party. I'm sorry for picking on you. You've been a great friend to me. Especially today."

Amanda started to smile. "The files have copied," she said. She turned her attention back to the computer screen.

Shawn loaded the app. He began to reassemble his project. He ordered the files from oldest to newest.

The entire room was almost all code.

"Shawn?" Amanda said. She sounded weird.

He looked at her.

She was turning into 0s and 1s.

"I have to tell you something." She adjusted her glasses. "About earlier today. When I saw you in Mr. Murphy's class, I didn't know who you were. Not at first."

"You didn't?" Shawn was starting to get scared. Maybe he couldn't get back to his old life. "Why did you act like you did?"

"I wasn't acting. The second you looked at me I knew. It was like I was meant to help you. Like we were meant to be friends. I've hated you because you're always late. You never get punished for anything. You have it so easy. Now I realize you don't," she cried. "It only seems that way. I'm sorry for being mean to you. I'm sorry ..."

Amanda disappeared. Poof!

"Amanda!" he called. He knew it would do no good.

The menu appeared.

EDIT

QWIK CUT

Shawn selected 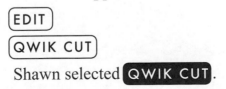 QWIK CUT .

Another screen came up. It was the export timeline. It told him how long it would take to finish.

Shawn squinted. He couldn't read the screen. Why not? Then he knew. Everything was turning into 0s and 1s. Including him.

Everything went black. Again.

CHAPTER 15

FADE OUT

Shawn woke up. His alarm clock was buzzing.

6:30 a.m.

"Shawn!" his mom called to him like always. "You're late again. You should've gotten up thirty minutes ago. Do not hit that snooze button again."

Normally Shawn would have stretched. Pulled his covers tight. Rolled over. His mom would come upstairs. She'd yell at him some more.

Not today.

Shawn sprang out of bed.

He looked around his bedroom. All his books. His clothes. His computer. All of his electronics were there! Everything was back to normal.

His computer was still on. Just like how he'd left it before the hacked app went crazy.

There was a message on his desktop. It was from *Qwik Cutter*.

> YOUR FILE HAS BEEN EXPORTED

It said 11 hrs/45 mins.

Using the mouse, Shawn grabbed the file. He dropped it into the trash. Then he deleted it from his computer forever.

"No more shortcuts. No more hacked programs," he said. "No more being late."

Then he deleted the hacked version. Good-bye, *Qwik Cutter*.

He threw on some jeans. Got a clean T-shirt. Brushed his teeth. He didn't shower. He just grabbed his backpack. Then ran out of the house. He would be on time for everything today.

He was the first student to arrive on campus

that morning. EJ was surprised. The security guard asked Shawn if he was feeling okay.

Shawn was first to all his classes.

Mr. Murphy looked oddly at Shawn as he walked into class.

"Man," John said when he got there. "What's the matter with you?"

"I don't know. I guess I don't want to be late anymore," Shawn said.

Nobody had any idea what had happened the day before. Nobody remembered not knowing Shawn. Nobody knew about the hacked program. Nobody knew about the world turning into code.

Maybe yesterday never happened.

"Mr. Miller," Mr. Murphy said, smiling. "Not only are you on time, you're early. I trust you have a masterpiece to show me. It's due today."

Shawn walked up to the teacher. "Well," he said nervously. "About that. Can I take a lower grade and upload it later today?"

"You want to turn it in late? You didn't get it done?"

"Um, I did finish," Shawn said. "There was a glitch with my editing program."

Mr. Murphy stared at him for a moment.

"Okay," the teacher finally said. "You can still get a B if you upload it by tonight. But it better be good."

"Thank you," Shawn said as he sat down. "It'll be good."

Other students started to walk into class. Shawn took out his iPad.

"You're on time!" Amanda said.

He looked her. He had been busy trying not to be late. He hadn't thought about her. He wondered now if she remembered.

She stared at him. She moved her glasses. Shawn knew then she had no idea what they had done together. He knew she didn't know how she had helped him. He also knew she didn't remember what she'd said before she turned into code.

"Okay," Mr. Murphy said, breaking into Shawn's thoughts. He was addressing the class. "Turn in your DVDs. Your flash drives. Or your SD cards. And thank you for uploading them last night if you did."

"Already turn in your project?" John asked as he took out his DVD.

"Not yet." Shawn smiled sheepishly.

"But I thought you used *Qwik Cutter*. It didn't work?"

"You could say that," Shawn said. "I guess I realized I shouldn't use a hacked program."

"That's just another excuse," Amanda hissed through gritted teeth. "You're always late, Shawn Miller. You'll always be late. People like you drag this world down!"

Amanda gave him a smug smile. She stood up. She turned in her DVD.

Shawn was mad. He was going to get Amanda. He didn't know how, but he would. Then he realized how petty that was. *I got my life back. And*

I'm not gonna waste a second. I'm gonna be on time. Because I don't want to miss anything important ever again.

Amanda stared at him as she sat down.

It was then that he noticed. *Amanda looks cute behind those glasses. When everything was in code? Maybe she helped me because she liked me. Deep down.*

He watched her as she took out her iPad.

Me and Amanda? No way! He smiled to himself as Mr. Murphy turned on the projector. *I guess this is one more reason to be on time for school.*

WANT TO KEEP READING?

9781680211085

Turn the page for a sneak
peek at another book in the
White Lightning series:

BREAK AND ENTER

CHAPTER 1

MY FIRST BREAK-IN

Lots of people have weird hobbies. Like bug collecting. Mine? Breaking and entering.

I'm not bad. I don't break in to take stuff. That's what you're thinking, right?

It started when we moved here. Me and my mom. This city is full of apartments. What was inside each one? I wanted to find out.

Because my life sucks.

I wanted to borrow another life for a while.

Pretend I'm someone else. Trade my reality for make-believe.

Even if it was just for an afternoon.

"We'll get used to this," my mom said. "It'll take time."

"Yeah. Well, I want my old life back. I miss my friends. I miss the sun," I complained.

"This is for the best," she said.

End of story. I knew we couldn't go back. But, man, life was hard.

She knows moving here was tough on me. On both of us. We moved to get away from my father. He's not a nice guy.

To me, my mom, or anybody.

He's in prison right now. We wanted to start over. So we moved east.

It's been rough. My old life in California was all I knew. I'm trying to fit in here. But it's taking a while.

Other people's lives seem better than mine. I'm ready to trade.

I saw the open window walking to school. Anyone could have crawled through. Who leaves a first-floor window open? Especially in this part of town.

Crazy. They were lucky I was the one who discovered it. Instead of someone bad.

Three days in a row it was open. It was like an itch I couldn't scratch. Had to get inside. Couldn't let it go.

I needed a plan.

1. Go in the middle of the day
2. Ditch school right after lunch
3. Think of a lie to tell Mom in case school calls
4. Walk back to the apartment with the open window

5. Check around back for more open windows
6. It there isn't one, try more windows
7. But first make sure the coast is clear
8. Important!!! Check for dogs

It was after lunch. Mom wouldn't find out I'd ditched school till later. Whatever. I'd make up something good. My mom is too trusting.

I walked to the apartment. Went around back. Didn't see any cars. But that doesn't mean anything. Most people take the bus to work.

The back gate squeaked. I freaked. Crouched down. Waited to see if anyone came out to investigate. After a minute I stood back up.

One window wouldn't move. Another had frosted glass. Hmm. The bathroom window? I pushed up against the frame. It moved up a couple inches.

"Here, boy! Come here, pup!" I called softly.

Lots of people here have dogs. No pit bull surprises, please. But no dog came.

No way could I pull myself up. It was too high.

There was a broken chair in the yard. I moved it under the window. It was the right height. I opened the window wider. Threw a leg over the windowsill. Shifted my weight. Pulled the other leg in. Dropped to the floor.

I was in.